The New Computer

Written by Antony Lishak

Illustrated by Sarah Warburton

Open the box.

nter
Keyboard

Where is the keyboard?

board

Where's the printer?

Printer

Where's the mouse?
Mouse

Where's Grandpa?

Turn it on.

Where's the picture?

Here's the plug!